Are You Awake?

Sophie Blackall

Christy Ottaviano Books
Henry Holt and Company
New York

Mom?

MMM?

Mom?

YES, EDWARD?

Mom, are you awake?

MM-MM. NO.

Why aren't you awake?

BECAUSE I'M ASLEEP.

Why are you asleep?

BECAUSE IT'S STILL NIGHTTIME.

Why is it still nighttime?

BECAUSE THE SUN HASN'T COME UP YET.

Why hasn't the sun come up yet?

BECAUSE THE STARS ARE STILL OUT.

Why are the stars still out?

BECAUSE IT'S NIGHTTIME.

Oh.

Can I have breakfast now?

No.

Why can't I?

BECAUSE WE'VE RUN OUT OF MILK.

Can we get some more?

No.

Why can't we?

BECAUSE THE CORNER STORE ISN'T OPEN YET.

Why isn't it open yet?

BECAUSE IT'S
STILL NIGHTTIME.

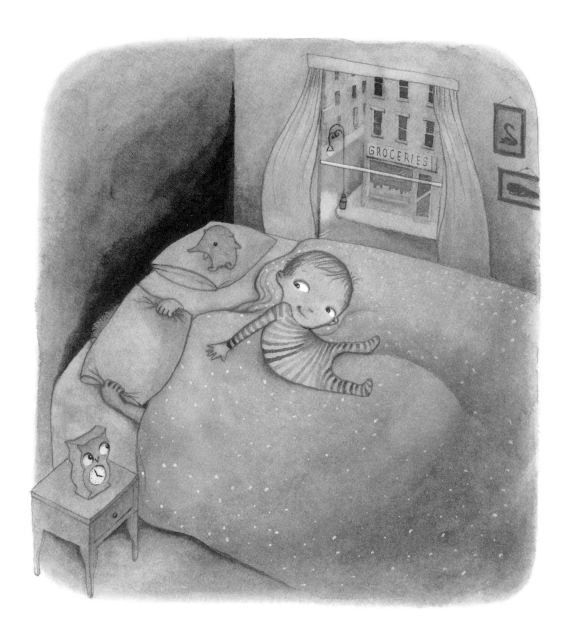

Why is it still nighttime?

BECAUSE THE SUN HASN'T COME UP YET.

Why hasn't the sun come up yet?

BECAUSE THE ALARM CLOCK HASN'T RUNG.

Why hasn't the alarm clock rung?

BECAUSE IT'S NIGHTTIME.

Oh.

Mom?

Mmm?

Is Daddy awake?

I hope so.

Why do you hope so?

Because he's flying a plane.

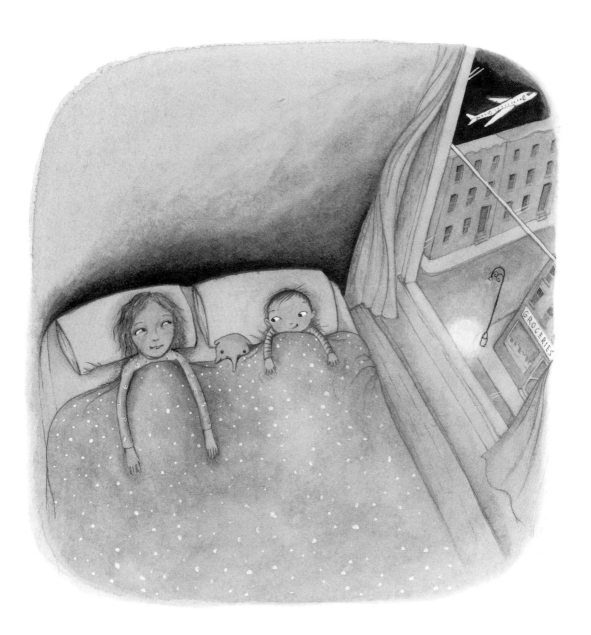

Why is he flying a plane?

TO TAKE THE PEOPLE WHERE THEY WANT TO GO.

But why do they want to go at night?

SO THEY CAN BE THERE IN THE MORNING.

Is it morning yet?

NO.

Why isn't it?

BECAUSE IT'S STILL NIGHTTIME.

Why is it still nighttime?

BECAUSE THE SUN HASN'T COME UP YET.

Why hasn't the sun come up yet?

BECAUSE THE MOON IS STILL OUT.

Why is the moon still out?

BECAUSE IT'S NIGHTTIME.

Oh.

Mom?

Yes?

Do you like yellow?

Yes, I like yellow. Do you like yellow?

Yes. It's my favorite color.

Why is it your favorite color?

Because there are lots of yellow things.

What are some yellow things?

Bananas are yellow. And taxis.
And I have a yellow rubber band.

WHAT ELSE?

Dogs are yellow.

NO, THEY'RE NOT.

Yellow dogs are.

Can you tell me some other yellow things?

WELL . . . SCHOOL BUSES AND CANARIES
ARE YELLOW. AN EGG YOLK IS YELLOW,
AND SO IS CHEESE AND CORN ON THE COB.
SOME THINGS COME IN YELLOW AS WELL
AS OTHER COLORS, LIKE T-SHIRTS AND SOCKS
AND BUILDING BLOCKS. SOME NAMES SOUND
YELLOW TO ME, LIKE PETER, AND SOME
LETTERS AND NUMBERS, LIKE E AND 3.
BUT DO YOU KNOW WHAT THE
YELLOWEST THING IS?

THE YELLOWEST THING IS THE MORNING
WHEN THE SUN COMES UP.

EDWARD?